Picture Folk-Tales

VALERY CARRICK

ILLUSTRATED BY THE AUTHOR

"The Child's joy is the world's joy"

DOVER PUBLICATIONS, INC.
New York

DOVER CHILDREN'S THRIFT CLASSICS

EDITOR: PHILIP SMITH

Published in Canada by General Publishing Company, Ltd., 30 Lesmill Road, Don Mills, Toronto, Ontario.

Published in the United Kingdom by Constable and Company, Ltd., 3 The Lanchesters, 162–164 Fulham Palace Road, London W6 9ER.

This Dover edition, first published in 1992, is an unabridged republication of the work originally published as *Valery Carrick's Picture Folk-Tales* by Frederick A. Stokes Company, New York, 1926. A new Note has been specially prepared for this edition.

Manufactured in the United States of America
Dover Publications, Inc., 31 East 2nd Street, Mineola, N.Y. 11501

Library of Congress Cataloging-in-Publication Data

Karrik, Valerian Vil'iamovich, 1869–1942.
    Picture folk-tales / Valery Carrick ; illustrated by the author.
        p.   cm. — (Dover children's thrift classics)
    Originally published: Valery Carrick's picture folk-tales. New York: Frederick A. Stokes Co., 1926.
    Summary: Ten Russian animal folk tales, including "The Tortoise and the Elephant," "The Ram and the Leopard," and "The Wolf's Dream."
    ISBN 0-486-27083-1 (pbk.)
    1. Tales—Soviet Union. [1. Folklore—Soviet Union. 2. Animals—Folklore.] I. Title. II. Title: Picture folk tales. III. Series.
PZ8.1.K149Ph   1992
398.24'52'0947—dc20
                                          91–37729
                                           CIP
                                           AC

Note to the Dover Edition

VALERY CARRICK was born Valerian Vil'iamovich Karrik in Russia in 1869. As a young boy, he heard many folk tales, spoken stories that had been passed down from generation to generation among the peasants of his native land. Many years later he wrote down the stories he had heard, and created simple drawings to accompany them.

These stories are similar to those told in many lands. They mainly concern animals, although these animals often speak and behave like people. These stories are similar in this respect to fables, which are brief tales designed to teach a simple lesson. As you read of the adventures of the lions, lambs, goats and elephants in this book, you may find that you learn something useful from their experiences.

CONTENTS

THE TORTOISE AND THE ELEPHANT

One day an elephant met a tortoise, and t h e tortoise said:

"What sort of little beast is that?"

"What! Little beast? Do you dare to call me a little beast?" said the elephant.

"Well, who are you, then, if you aren't a little beast?" asked the tortoise.

"I'm the biggest of all the beasts in the whole forest," answered the elephant. "I have no equal in strength or in swiftness."

"The biggest of all the beasts in the forest?" said the tortoise. "But I could jump over you if I liked!"

"You? Jump over me?" said the elephant. "You just try!"

"Very well, I will. Only today I am a bit tired. I have walked a long way. Come tomorrow to this same place, and you'll see, I'll jump over you!"

"Right," said the elephant. "I'll be here!"

The next day the tortoise and the elephant met again at the same place.

Now the tortoise, as you know, is a cunning creature. She had asked her sister to come, too, and hide in the grass. And the elephant said:

"Well, Miss Tortoise, are you going to start jumping?"

"I am!" replied she. "You just stand

quite still, and I'll jump from this side over onto the other!"

And the elephant stood still, and the tortoise pretended that she was going to

jump, and all the time her sister was hidden in the grass on the other side.

"Look out!" shouted the tortoise. "Hop!"

At that the elephant turned round to the other side, and there was the tortoise's sister poking her head out of the grass and saying:

"Here I am!"

And the elephant was greatly astonished and said:

"Well, now, jump back again!"

"All right!" answered the tortoise. "Hop!"

The elephant turned round again, and behold, there was the tortoise back again exactly where it was before. And the elephant was still more astonished, and said:

"Well, really, you are good at jumping, and no mistake. Let's see you do it again!"

"Hop!" cried the tortoise. And the elephant turned round, and there was the tortoise again on the other side.

"Once again!" he shouted.

"Hop!" cried the tortoise, and again ap-

peared in the same place as in the beginning.

The elephant felt quite ashamed. He
had no idea the tortoise was so clever at
jumping, and he said:

"Well, you were quite right! I can see
you are very good at jumping. But of
course running is quite another matter! And
you must excuse my saying so, but you
are quite hopeless at that! In fact, you're
the slowest of all the beasts in the world!"

"Hee-hee!" laughed the tortoise. "Evidently you don't know me at all! I can run a race with anybody and win!"

"Very well!" said the elephant. "Let's have a race as far as that tree over there!"

"It's all very well for you!" replied the tortoise. "You haven't been jumping! I have, and I'm quite tired. Come along tomorrow, and then we'll have a running race. You'll see, I'll beat you!"

The next day the tortoise collected all her relations, all her brothers and sisters, all her uncles and aunts, and said to them:

"Go and hide in the grass at intervals from here to that tree over there."

And all the tortoise's relations went and hid in the grass.

Presently the elephant came up and said:

"Well, Miss Tortoise, are we going to run our race?"

"Of course! Why not?" replied she. "You just stand alongside of me!"

And they went and stood side by side.

"Ready. Steady. Go!" cried the tortoise, and the elephant started off running, but the tortoise crouched down in the grass. And the elephant went on running, running, and thought:

"Well, I must have left the tortoise a long way behind by now!"

Then he stopped and shouted:

"Miss Tortoise, Miss Tortoise, where are you?"

And her brother answered from out of the grass:

"Here I am! Why have you stopped?"

Then the elephant started off running again, and he ran and ran, and at last stopped and asked:

"Where are you, Miss Tortoise?"

And the tortoise's aunt replied from out of the grass:

"Here I am! Why don't you go on running?"

The elephant saw that the tortoise kept ahead of him all the time, so he made a tremendous effort, put forth all his strength, and ran on as fast as he could. At last he got to the tree and thought:

"Well, now I must surely have overtaken her! Where are you, Miss Tortoise?" he asked.

And the tortoise's uncle answered from out of the grass:

"I've been waiting for you here a long time!"

And the elephant was more surprised than ever and said to himself:

"Well, that's some tortoise!" and went home very angry.

THE ELEPHANT AND THE WHALE

One day a hare and a jackal set off on a journey together. After a bit they came to the seashore, and there they saw an elephant  standing and talking to a whale.

The elephant said:

"Look here, Brother Whale, you are the strongest beast in the sea, and I'm the strongest in the forest. Let's agree to rule all the other beasts—you, those in the water, and I, those on land. And if any one doesn't obey us, we'll wipe him off the face of the earth."

"Right," answered the whale; "we will."

When he heard this, the jackal was frightened, and said to the hare:

"Do you hear what they are saying? We'd better be off, or else we shall get into trouble for having listened to what they were saying."

But the hare said in reply:

"What are you afraid of? Do you really believe, just because they are big and strong, they can rule over every one else? Just you watch and see me make fools of them."

Then the hare got a long rope, took one end, and went up to the elephant and said:

"Sir, you are so big and strong, and I'm told you are very kind, too! Please help me; I'm in great trouble! My cow was

grazing quietly, when she got into the marsh, and I simply can't pull her out!"

The elephant was very pleased at being called powerful and kind, and said:

"Of course, I'll be only too glad to help you, Mr. Hare! Tell me where your cow is?"

"She's deep in the marsh," answered the

hare. "You can't see her; you can only see her two horns sticking out! I'll go and fasten the other end of the rope to her horns, and then, when I start beating the drum, you start pulling."

"All right," said the elephant; "go and fasten the rope."

Then the hare took the other end of the rope, and went off to the whale, and said:

"Oh, Mr. Whale! There's no fish in the sea, no beast in the forest, no bird in the air that can compare with you in strength! Please help me in my trouble!"

The whale was very pleased at being told he was held greater than all the other beasts and birds, and he said:

"Certainly I will! What is the matter?"

"My cow was quietly grazing," said the hare, "when she sank in the marsh! I struggled and struggled to get her out,

but it was no use! Do please be kind and help me out of my trouble! Here's a rope, you see; you take one end, and I'll fasten the other end to the cow's horns. Then, when I start beating the drum, you just give ever such a slight pull, and you're bound to pull her out!"

"Right!" answered the whale. "I will!"

Then the hare went off, stopped half-way between the two, and started beating the drum. And the elephant began to pull, and the whale began to pull! First of all they pulled quite gently, and the rope just got taut. Then they began to pull harder, and the rope got as taut as a string on a bow!

"How very extraordinary!" thought the elephant. "Surely that cow can't have sunk so deep that I can't pull her out!"

And he made a great effort, and started pulling the whale towards the shore.

And the whale thought:

"Well, this hare must have an uncommonly large cow! Surely I shall be able to pull her out! All the beasts will start making fun of me!"

And then he made a great effort, and started pulling the elephant, and he pulled him right up to the seashore.

"Well, I never! Is that you, Brother Elephant?" he then exclaimed.

"Well, I never! Is that you, Brother Whale?" answered the elephant.

"Well, a pretty pair of fools the hare has made of us!" they said together.

And Mr. Hare had vanished.

THE OWL, THE FOX AND THE CROW

An owl once built a nest in a tree-hollow, and laid some eggs, and began to raise her baby owls. And the fox heard about this, and thought he would like to see what the owl's children tasted like.

So he went up to the oak in which the owl's nest was and went *thud-thud* with his tail against the oak-tree. At that the owl looked out and asked:

"What are you doing, Mr. Fox?"

"I'm going to cut down the oak," replied he.

"What do you want the oak for?" asked the owl.

"To make some runners for my sled," said the fox.

"Don't cut down the oak, Mr. Fox; I'm bringing up my children in it," said the owl.

"And do you think I'm going to go about on foot just because of your children?" asked the fox.

"Oh, just wait a week, Mr. Fox, and let my children get out of their shells," said the owl.

"All right, I will," replied the fox, and went away.

And he came again in a week's time, and started to go *thud-thud* with his tail against the green oak-tree. And the owl said:

"What are you doing, Mr. Fox?"

And he replied:

"I'm going to cut down the oak-tree."

"What do you want the oak-tree for?" asked the owl.

"To make some runners for my sled," answered the fox.

"Don't cut down the oak-tree, Mr. Fox. I have my children in the nest here," said the owl.

"And do you think I'm going to go about on foot just because of your children?" said the fox.

"Just wait a week," said the owl, "and let them grow a little bigger."

"Oh, very well," said the fox, and went away.

At that moment the owl heard some one making a noise on the oak-tree, and she got very frightened and asked:

"Who's there?"

"It's I, the crow," came the answer.

"What on earth are you frightened of, Mrs. Owl?"

"Oh, Mr. Fox has just been here, starting to cut down the oak-tree. That's why I got frightened. I thought he had come back again," said the owl.

"Well, but no fox has ever been seen to

cut down an oak-tree, Mrs. Owl!" said the crow. "Next time the fox comes along just you tell him: 'You can't do it, sir,' and no more! And you yourself keep sitting still; don't be afraid."

Presently along came the fox once more,

and went *thud-thud* against the oak-tree with his tail. So the owl said from out of her nest:

"What are you doing, Mr. Fox?"

"I'm going to cut down the oak-tree," answered he.

"You can't do it, sir. I am not afraid!" said the owl. "Has a fox ever been seen to cut down an oak-tree with his tail, I should like to know!"

At this the fox saw that there was **no** hope of fooling the owl, so he asked:

"And who was it put you up to that, Mrs. Owl?"

"Mrs. Crow did," answered the owl.

"Oh, did she! Very well, I'll just pay her for that!" said the fox.

Then he went a little distance away from the tree, lay down on the ground, and never moved, pretending to be dead.

Presently the crow came flying along,

and saw the fox there, lying still. So she flew to the ground, hopped up to one side of the fox, and asked:

"Are you dead or alive, Mr. Fox?"

And the fox said never a word.

Then the crow hopped up to his other side, and said:

"Foxy, speak up, if you're alive!"

But the fox made never a sound! So the crow thought: "Well, the fox really must be dead!" and, plucking up courage, hopped right onto the fox, when—bang he went with his paws, and spun the crow to the earth!

"Now, just you look here, my friend," said he, "I'm going to pay you back for putting Mrs. Owl up to that trick!"

Then the crow began to implore him, saying:

"Oh, Foxy dear, please kill me at once.

Don't let me die the way my father did!"

"And how was that?" asked the fox.

"Well," said the crow, "they caught him just as you caught me, and put him in a sieve, and then started rolling him along, and they rolled him and rolled him till he died!"

"Right, then," answered the fox; "your death shall be the same!"

And the fox got a sieve, put the crow in it, and starting rolling her along,

when—the crow just fluttered out of the sieve and escaped!

Then she flew up to the oak-tree and started crying:

"I got the better of you! I got the better of you!"

THE THREE BRUZE GOATS

Once upon a time there were three goats, and they were all named Bruze.

One day they thought they would like to go up to the hill meadows, to nibble the nice fresh grass, that grows there, and get a little more flesh and fat on their bones.

And so the youngest led the way. And

the road lay across a bridge, and under t h a t bridge there dwelt a horrible goblin, as fat as a balloon, with eyes as big as saucers and a nose like a poker. And the little goat

started to go over the bridge: TRIP-TRAP, TRIP-TRAP, TRIP-TRAP!

And the goblin said from under the bridge:

"Who is that walking over my bridge with such quite little steps?"

"It is I, the youngest Bruze goat. I'm off to the hills to have a good feed," answered the little goat.

"Oh, I'm going to eat you!" said the goblin.

"No, don't eat me, goblin, please!" answered the goat. "I'm very small and thin. My elder brother will be coming along presently; he's bigger than I."

"Oh, all right, then," said the goblin, and settled himself to sleep again under his bridge.

[29]

Then the middle Bruze goat came up to the bridge: TRIP-TRAP, TRIP-TRAP, TRIP-TRAP!

And the goblin asked:

"Who is that walking over my bridge, tapping so with his feet?"

"It's I, the middle Bruze goat," answered he. "I'm off to the hills to have a good feed."

"Oh, I'm going to eat you!" said the goblin.

"Don't eat me, goblin, please!" answered the goat. "I'm quite small. But my eldest brother is coming along after me, and he's bigger than I."

"Oh, all right, then!" said the goblin.

And presently the eldest Bruze goat came along: **TRIP-TRAP, TRIP-TRAP, TRIP-TRAP!**

And the goblin asked:

"Who is that walking over my bridge

in such a funny way, knocking and stamp-
ing and thumping?"

"It's I, the eldest Bruze goat," answered
he. "I'm off to the hills to have a good
feed."

"Oh, I'm going to eat you!" said the
goblin, and was just going to seize hold
of him, when the goat took a run and
butted him with his horns, and the goblin
flew head-over-heels under the bridge, right

down to the bottom of the gully—and that
was the end of him.

And the three Bruze goats grazed all
summer up in the hills, got a lot of flesh
and fat on their bones, and came home as
plump as plump could be.

THE RAM AND THE LEOPARD

Once upon a time a ram thought he would build himself a house in the forest. So he went into the woods and made a clearing.

"That's done now," he said; "tomorrow I'll have a rest, and after that I'll start building my house."

Then he went back to his home.

But at the same time a leopard thought he would build himself a house in the forest. So he went there and began to look for a likely place, when suddenly he saw that a clearing had already been made, as though on purpose for a house to be built there.

"That's splendid!" he thought. "I'll begin to build my house here!"

And he started dragging sticks and

stakes and logs along. He worked all day, and got very tired, and then he said:

"Well, the beginning is always the hardest part. Tomorrow I'll rest, and then start work again!"

The next day the ram came along, and saw all the sticks and stakes and logs gathered there—all he had to do was to put them together! And he was very much surprised, and he thought:

"This must be the fairies helping me!"

And then he began putting the walls up. And he got half-way, and then felt very tired, so he went away to rest.

The next day the leopard came along again, and saw that the walls had been half built, and he thought:

"There, isn't that splendid! I had a rest yesterday, and the fairies meantime helped me!"

And he started to work and finished

building the walls, and got very tired, and thought:

"That's all right! All tomorrow I'll rest, and then I'll finish it off!"

The next day the ram came along, and saw that it was all done except the roof. And he set to work and put the roof on. Then he thought:

"Well, tomorrow I'll just have a good rest, and then I can start moving in!"

The next day the leopard came along

again, and when he saw what had happened he thought:

"There now, would you believe it, the work's finished! The roof is on! Tomorrow I'll move in!"

The next day the ram started moving into his new house, and the leopard also started moving into his new house, and they both came along and met, and the ram said:

"This house is for *me* to live in! I built

it, and the fairies came and helped me!"

But the leopard said:

"No! This house is for *me* to live in! It was *I* who built it, and the fairies came and helped *me*!"

And they argued about it for a long time, and couldn't settle who was to live in the house, or whom the fairies had helped. And in the end they went for judgment to the lion, and said to him:

"Please, will you decide the question: Who built the house, whom did the fairies help, and who is to live in it?"

And the lion replied:

"Both of you built the house and the fairies helped you both, and so both of you go and live in it, and don't quarrel!"

So both the leopard and the ram started living in the house, and they got on all right and didn't quarrel. The leopard would go off hunting, bring back his prey and eat it. And the ram just kept on walking about round the house, nibbling the grass and getting quite satisfied with that.

And the leopard began to wonder how it was: the ram had no sharp teeth, had no claws, and besides that he was lazy, so how did he manage to get plenty to eat and keep fat? How did he catch his prey? So he asked him one day:

"How do you catch your prey, Mr. Ram?"

And the ram answered:

"How do I catch my prey? First of all you show me how you catch *your* prey!"

Then the leopard put a log of wood on the ground, and began to approach it as if he were hunting. First he'd come up from one side, crouch down on the earth and creep along; then he'd come up from the other side, crouch down on the earth

and creep along. Then all at once he'd spring right onto the log and start gnawing it with his teeth, hitting it with his paws, and tearing it with his claws.

And the ram watched him and then said:

"Well, now I'll show you how I catch *my* prey."

And he went and stood in front of the log, and then began to back. And he

backed and backed, till all at once he ran forward at the log and butted it hard with his horns, and the log went spinning away like a top.

So the leopard saw that the ram was very strong, and he thought to himself:

"The ram's a dangerous beast! I must be on the lookout, or he'll do for me. But there's one good thing: I know he's got to go back before he comes forward!"

And after that they went on living happily, the leopard going off hunting and bringing back his prey, and the ram walking around the house and nibbling the grass. But the leopard kept a sharp lookout and watched to see if the ram had started backing.

Then came the rains, and the earth got wet and slippery. And one day the leopard and the ram were standing together when suddenly the ram slipped, and he slipped so much that he went quite a long way back.

And when the leopard saw this he was terribly frightened and thought:

"O dear, O dear! My end has come!"

And with that he dashed off into the forest. And ever since then the ram has been sole master of the house.

THE WOLF'S DREAM

Once upon a time a wolf and a fox stole a hen, and they hid it away for the next day's dinner and went to bed.

And the fox went to sleep, but the wolf didn't, but lay awake thinking: "Shall I eat the hen now while the fox is asleep, and then dream dreams about it and lick my chops in memory of the feast I had, or shall I first go to sleep and dream dreams about the hen, and then eat it?"

And he kept on revolving these thoughts in his head; first of all he thought the first way was better, then he thought the second way wasn't bad either. And at last he fell asleep in the midst of these thoughts.

Then the fox woke up and saw that the wolf was asleep. So he went close up to

the hen and sat down in front of it, and thought to himself:

"Shall I eat the wing or the leg? The leg or the wing?"

At last he decided to eat the wing, and when he had eaten it he thought:

"The hen's wing is certainly delicious, but I should be surprised if the leg were not still more so. I think I'll now eat the leg!"

And when he had finished the leg, he thought:

"After all, I think the wing was nicer! Now shall I eat the other wing or the other leg?"

And after a great deal of thought he ate the other wing. And when he had eaten it he thought to himself again:

"Well, what's the good now of leaving the other leg? I may as well eat that too!"

And so he ate the other leg, as well.

And when he had eaten it he lay down to sleep. And he turned and turned, from one side to the other, but couldn't get a wink of sleep. And there in front of him was still the body of the hen. And he got up and went up to it again and said:

"Why do you lie there like that, wingless and legless, and keep me from going to sleep?"

And the fox ate up the whole body of

the hen. Only the feathers were left. Then he sprinkled the feathers over the wolf's muzzle and lay down to sleep.

And the wolf slept the whole time and kept seeing the hen in his dreams and thought he was eating it.

Next morning when he woke up he saw that there was no hen. The fox was fast asleep, and he waked the fox saying:

"Mr. Fox, Mr. Fox, wake up!"

"What do you want, Mr. Wolf?" answered the fox.

"Where's our hen, I should like to know?" asked the wolf.

At this the fox jumped up and opened his eyes very, very wide, and said:

"I do believe you have eaten it, Mr. Wolf! Just look, all your muzzle is covered with feathers!"

The wolf was very much surprised at this and said:

"Well, I never; my muzzle is covered with feathers! I suppose I must have eaten it in my sleep! But the extraordinary thing is, I've eaten a whole hen, and yet my stomach feels quite empty. I can't understand it!"

THE GOLDEN FISH

Once upon a time there lived an old couple. The old woman used to spin yarn and the old man used to catch fish.

One day he went to the seashore and cast his net into the sea. When he pulled it out, there was nothing in it, except sand and stones. So he cast it a second time; and again he got nothing except mud and weeds. Then he cast it a third time, and he started pulling and pulling, and found that the net was coming in very slowly.

At last he pulled it into the boat, and there in the net was a golden fish!

And the fish began to beg of the old man:

"Let me go back into the sea! I will give you any ransom you like!"

And the old man thought to himself: "What good is the fish to me? I'll let it go for nothing!"

So he let it go back into the sea.

Then he came home to his wife and she asked him:

"Have you brought any fish for dinner?"

"No, I haven't," he answered. "The first time I pulled out the net, there were only sand and stones. The second time, only mud and weeds. Then I cast it a third time, and caught a golden fish in it.

And the fish began to beg me to let it go, saying it would give me anything I liked; so I took it and let it go back into the sea!"

"Oh, you silly, you silly!" said his wife. "At least you might have asked for some ransom from it, such as a new trough. You know well enough that ours is all

cracked. Go to the sea, now, and ask the fish to give us a new trough!"

So the old man went off to the sea and began to call the golden fish:

"Golden fish, fish of gold, turn your head towards me, and your tail towards the sea!"

And the fish came swimming up out of the deep sea, and turned its head towards the old man and its tail towards the sea, saying:

"What do you want, old man?"

And he answered:

"Please give my wife a new trough. Ours is all cracked."

"Very well," said the fish. "You'll have a new trough all right. Good-by!"

So the old man went home, and there, lo and behold! stood a new trough.

But the old woman only said to her husband:

"Is that anything so wonderful? Fancy asking only for a new trough! Just go back to the fish and ask it to give us a new cottage!"

At this her husband started scratching his head, but presently he went back to the sea and said:

"Golden fish, fish of gold, turn your head towards me and your tail towards the sea!"

And the fish swam up again and asked:

"Well, old man, what have you come for now? What is it you want?"

"It isn't for me," answered he. "It's my wife who wants something. She wants a new cottage."

"All right, she shall have a new cottage," said the fish. "Good-by!"

And when he got back home, there was the new cottage, with a smooth timber gate and a carved wooden porch, and he asked his wife:

"Well, are you satisfied now?"

But she only said:

"Go back to the fish once more, and say that I don't want to be a simple peasant's wife; I want to be a grand lady, with lots of servants to do all my bidding."

So the old man again went off to the sea and started calling the fish:

"Golden fish, fish of gold, turn your

head towards me and your tail towards the sea!"

And the fish came swimming up and asked:

"Well, old man, what is it you want now?"

And he answered:

"My wife's getting foolish ideas in her head! She says she doesn't want to be a peasant's wife, but a grand lady, with lots of servants to do all her bidding."

"Very well," said the fish; "your wife shall be a grand lady. Good-by!"

And when the old man got home, he saw a big house where his cottage had been, and, inside, his wife sitting on soft cushions, and servants all around her handing her delicate food and foaming drinks, and she said angrily to him:

"What do you want here? You can go and live in the stables!"

So he went off to the stables and started living there.

After two days his wife sent for him to come to her in the house, and when he got there she said:

"Go at once to the golden fish, and say that I don't want to be just a grand lady; I want to be a queen, and for all to bow down and do me homage."

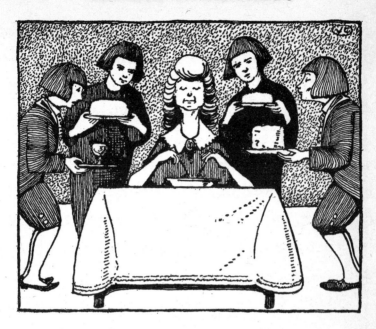

At this the old man stared with sur-
prise, but there was no help for it, so he
went off once more to the sea and started
calling the fish:

"Golden fish, fish of gold, turn your tail
towards the sea and your head towards
me!"

And the fish came swimming along and asked:

"What, has your wife sent you here again?"

"Yes," answered the old man. "She has sent me to you with her compliments and says she doesn't want to be just a grand lady, she wants to be a queen, and for all to bow down and pay her homage."

"Well," said the fish, "your wife shall be a queen. Good-by."

And when he got home, he saw that the house was no longer there, but in its place there stood a palace with pinnacles of gold, and all round it soldiers on sentry-guard, and his wife inspecting them, and all the people bowing down and paying her homage.

He didn't dare so much as show himself to her, but crept back to the stables and went on living there.

After a week or two, his wife sent for

him to come and see her in the palace.
And when he got there, she shouted at
him:

"Go and run quickly to the fish and
say that I'm tired of being a queen. I
want to be mistress of the sea and to have
the golden fish come and be my servant
and do all my bidding."

The old man didn't dare to argue, so he just went to the seashore again and called the fish:

"Golden fish, fish of gold, turn your tail towards the sea and your head towards me!"

But for a long time there was no fish to be seen, only the sea lashing and splashing, and the waves all tumbling and

running after one another. At last the fish
came swimming up and asked:

"What do you want, old man?"

"Don't be angry, fish, please," answered
he. "I don't know what to do with my
wife! She told me to come and tell you
that she wants to be mistress of the sea
and to have the golden fish come and be
her servant and do all her bidding."

To this the fish said never a word, but just turned its tail and swam off into the deep sea.

The old man stood there for a bit, waiting, and then at last wended his way home. When he got there, lo and behold! there stood the cottage as before, with his wife sitting on the earth-bank in front of it, and the broken trough by her side.

WHY HARES HAVE LONG EARS

Once upon a time a hare made friends with a sheep, and they started living and sharing everything together.

One day the sheep said to the hare:

"Let's build a house!"

"Let's!" answered the hare.

So off they went into the forest for some logs. They came up to a tree and the sheep said:

"I'll knock this tree down!"

"You'll never!" said the hare.

"Oh, but I will. I'll just show you!" answered the sheep.

And he took a long run, and went crash! into the tree with his horns, and the tree fell down.

And the hare said to himself: "So that's the way to knock trees down! Now I shall be able to do the same!"

And they came to another tree, and the hare said:

"I'll knock this tree down!"

"You'll never!" said the sheep.

"Oh, but I will. I'll just show you!" answered the hare.

And he took a long run, and went crash! into the tree with his forehead!

And the tree still stood where it was before but the hare's head had gone right into his shoulders.

The sheep saw that he must get the hare's head out from his shoulders, and he caught hold of the hare by the ears and began to pull. He pulled and pulled, till

at last the hare cried: "Stop!"

But the sheep still went on pulling. He pulled the hare's head back to its proper place, and his ears way out from his head!

And that's why hares have long ears.

THE CRAB AND THE JAGUAR

One day a crab sat on a stone and was having a game with his eyes. He would say to them:

"Eyes, little eyes of mine! Fly away to the blue sea, quick-quick-quick-quick-quick!"

And the eyes would leap from his head and fly off to the blue sea. Then he would say:

"Eyes, little eyes of mine! Fly back to me from the blue sea, quick-quick-quick-quick-quick!"

Then his eyes would come flying back and settle down again in their proper place. And in this way the crab used to play endless games and keep himself amused.

One day a jaguar came to that place

and looked at the crab and was very much astonished and said:

"Whatever are you doing, my friend?"

"What am I doing?" repeated the crab. "I'm just having a game with my eyes. I tell them to fly away, and they fly away. Then I tell them to fly back, and they come back to their proper place."

"What a wonderful thing!" said the jaguar. "Do, please, do it again!"

"All right!" answered the crab. "I will. Eyes, little eyes of mine! Fly away to the blue sea, quick-quick-quick-quick-quick!"

And his eyes flew away. Then he said:

"Eyes, little eyes of mine! Fly back from the blue sea, quick-quick-quick-quick-quick!"

And his eyes flew back and settled in their proper place.

"What a lovely game that is!" said the

jaguar. "Tell me, could you play it with my eyes?"

"Well, yes, I could," answered the crab; "but you know, just now, the terrible Animale-Podole, father of the Trahira-fish, is swimming about in the blue sea, and I'm very much afraid he might eat your eyes!"

"Oh, I don't suppose he will! Anyway, I'll risk it! Come, now, do make my eyes fly away!"

"Very well, I will!" said the crab. "Eyes of Mr. Jaguar! Fly away to the blue sea, quick-quick-quick-quick-quick!"

And the eyes leapt out of the jaguar's head and flew off to the blue sea. Then the jaguar said:

"Now tell them to come back again!"

"Eyes of Mr. Jaguar!" said the crab. "Fly back here from the blue sea, quick-quick-quick-quick-quick!"

And his eyes came flying back and settled again in their proper place. And the jaguar said:

"Oh, but you know that's really wonderfully funny! Please do it again!"

"Mind!" answered the crab. "I've told you the terrible Animale-Podole, father of the Trahira-fish, is swimming about in the sea. If he does eat up your eyes you'll be left without any!"

"Oh, never mind. Please do it again!" said the jaguar.

"Very well," answered the crab. "Eyes of Mr. Jaguar! Fly away to the blue sea, quick-quick-quick-quick-quick!"

And the jaguar's eyes flew off again to the blue sea. And it so happened that just in that spot and just at that time, the terrible Animale-Podole, father of the Trahira-fish, was swimming about, and he saw

the eyes of the jaguar and swallowed them. Then the crab called them back again:

"Eyes of Mr. Jaguar! Fly back from the blue sea, quick-quick-quick-quick-quick!"

But the eyes never flew back. And the

crab called them again and again; but it was no good. The terrible Animale-Podole, father of the Trahira-fish, had eaten them! And the jaguar got very angry with the crab and wanted to kill him, but couldn't catch him, for the crab crept under the stone. So there was no help for it, and the jaguar went off without his eyes. And after he had been walking a long time he met a King-vulture. And the King-vulture said to the jaguar:

"Where are you going, my friend?"

"I don't know where I'm going; that's just it!" replied the jaguar. "The crab sent my eyes away to the blue sea, and there the terrible Animale-Podole, father of the Trahira-fish, swallowed them. So now

I have to go about without eyes! Couldn't you make me some new ones?"

"Well, yes, I can! But you must make a promise and keep it: whatever beast you kill while hunting, always give me a share!"

"I promise!" said the jaguar.

So the King-vulture made the jaguar some new eyes, even better than his old ones. And ever since then, whatever beast the jaguar kills while out hunting, he always leaves a piece for the King-vulture.

THE FOX WHO ASKED FOR
A NIGHT'S LODGING

A fox was walking along a road and found a lost-shoe. He picked it up and went on into the village. There he came up to a peasant and said to him:

"Mr. Peasant, let me stay the night at your hut."

"But we're packed tight, as it is," answered he.

"Oh, I don't want much room, do I? I'll get on a bench, curl my tail underneath, and put the lost-shoe under the stove," said the fox.

So the peasant let him in. And he lay down on a bench, curled his tail underneath, and put the lost-shoe under the stove.

Early the next morning the fox got up, burnt his lost-shoe, and then began to ask:

"What have they done with my lost-shoe? A whole goose would hardly be enough to give me in return for it!"

There was nothing to be done, and the peasant did give him a goose in return for his shoe. So the fox took the goose and started off singing:

"Master Fox found a lost-shoe,
And got a goose in return for it!"

Presently, evening came on and the fox began to knock at the hut of another peasant: Knock-knock-knock!

"Who's there?" they asked.

"I, Mr. Fox," replied he. "Let me in to stay the night!"

"We're packed very tight, as it is," came the answer.

"Oh, I shan't make THAT any worse," said the fox. "I'll get on a bench, curl my tail underneath, and put the goose under the stove!"

So they agreed, and let the fox in. He lay down on a bench, curled his tail underneath, and put the goose under the stove.

Early the next morning he ate up the goose, and then said:

"But where's my goose? I don't know that I'd take even as much as a whole turkey in return for it!"

So the peasant gave him a turkey in return for his goose. Then the fox went off singing:

"Mr. Fox found
   a lost-shoe,
For his lost-
   shoe he got
   goose,
For his goose he got a turkey!"

Knock-knock-knock! he rapped again at the hut of a third peasant.

"Who's there?" they asked.

"I, Brother Fox. Let me in to stay the night!" said the fox.

"But we're tightly packed ourselves!" answered they.

"I shan't make THAT any worse. I'll get on a bench, curl my tail underneath, and put the turkey under the stove," said the fox.

So they let him in. And the fox lay down on a bench, curled his tail underneath, and put the turkey under the stove.

In the morning he got up, plucked the turkey and ate it. Then he said:

"Where's my turkey? A sheep would

hardly be enough to give me in return for it!"

There was nothing to be done, and

the peasant gave him a sheep in return for his turkey. Then the fox led away the sheep, and went along, singing:

"Mr. Fox found a lost-shoe,
For the shoe he got a goose,

For the goose he got a turkey,
For the turkey he got a sheep!"

At evening he knocked at a fourth hut.
"Who's there?" they asked.

"It's I, Brother Fox," answered he. "Let me in to stay the night!"

"But we're tightly packed enough, without you!" said they.

"I shan't make THAT any worse. I'll get on a bench, curl my tail underneath, and put the sheep under the stove," said the fox.

So they let him in. And the fox lay down on the bench, curled his tail underneath, and put the sheep under the stove.

Early the next morning he got up and ate the sheep, and then said:

"Where's my sheep? A

young wife would hardly be enough to give me in return!"

There was no help for it, and the peasant saw he would have to give one of his daughters to the fox, so he asked:

"But how are you going to carry her?"

"Oh, you just put her in a sack!" answered he.

So the peasant went and put a

DOG in a sack. And the fox picked up the sack and started off on his way. He went on and on, till suddenly he began to feel sort of weary, and laid down the sack and said:

"Wifey, sing me a song!"

At that the dog in the sack just gave a tremendous GROWL! And the fox took fright, ran off as quick as he could into the forest, and vanished in an instant.